CELEBRATE - CELEBRAMOS
CINCO DE MAYO

Marisa Boan

Most people think that Cinco de Mayo celebrates Mexico's Independence Day, however this is not true.

La mayoría de la gente piensa que el Cinco de Mayo celebra el Día de la Independencia de México, sin embargo, esto no es cierto.

Mexico's Independence Day is celebrated each year on September 16th. This is the date when Mexico declared its independence from Spain back in 1810.

El Día de la Independencia de México se celebra cada año el 16 de septiembre. Esta es la fecha en que México declaró su independencia de España en 1810.

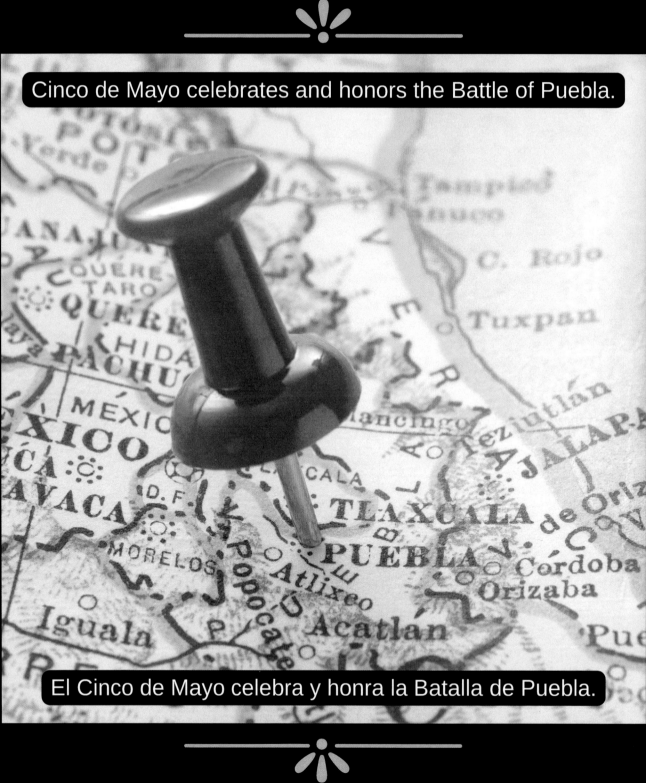

Cinco de Mayo celebrates and honors the Battle of Puebla.

El Cinco de Mayo celebra y honra la Batalla de Puebla.

On May 5, 1862 an important battle took place in the small town of Puebla between Mexico and France. France attacked Mexico in 1862 in the hopes of making Mexico a French colony.

El 5 de mayo de 1862 tuvo lugar una importante batalla en la pequeña ciudad de Puebla entre México y Francia. Francia atacó a México en 1862 con la esperanza de hacer de México una colonia francesa.

A Mexican army of about 4,500 soldiers battled with the larger and better equipped French army of about 6,000 soldiers. The Mexican soldiers were outnumbered, but still they fought hard and drove the French army out of Mexico.

Un ejército mexicano de unos 4.500 soldados luchó con el ejército francés más grande y mejor equipado de unos 6.000 soldados. Los soldados mexicanos fueron superados en número, pero aún así lucharon duro y expulsaron al ejército francés de México.

The victory of the Battle of Puebla is celebrated each year on May 5th. Many people celebrate this holiday in Mexico and in the United States.

La victoria de la Batalla de Puebla se celebra cada año el 5 de mayo. Muchas personas celebran esta fiesta en México y en los Estados Unidos.

Each year there are big celebrations! The fiestas include parades, carnivals,and performers in traditional costumes, while Mariachi bands fill the air with music and songs.

¡Cada año hay grandes celebraciones! Las fiestas incluyen desfiles, carnavales e intérpretes con trajes tradicionales, mientras que las bandas de mariachi llenan el aire c on música y canciones.

This is a time of great pride for the Mexican people!

¡Este es un momento de gran orgullo para el pueblo mexicano!

Cinco de Mayo has become a bigger holiday in the United States than in many places in Mexico.

Cinco de Mayo incluso se ha convertido en una fiesta más grande en los Estados Unidos que en lugares de México.

In many states like California, Texas, Arizona, and New Mexico, special events and celebrations take place during the week of May 5th.

En muchos estados como California, Texas, Arizona y Nuevo México, eventos especiales y celebraciones tienen lugar durante la semana del 5 de mayo.

In cities with large Mexican populations there are street festivals and parades. Some cities stage reenactments of the battle where men dress up as Mexican and French soldiers.

En las ciudades con grandes poblaciones mexicanas hay festivales callejeros y desfiles. Algunas ciudades escenifican recreaciones de la batalla donde los hombres se visten de soldados mexicanos y franceses.

Delicious food is a huge part of the celebration, and not just tacos.

Deliciosa comida es una gran parte de la celebración, y no sólo tacos.

People look forward to feasting on traditional Mexican dishes like mole poblano and chalupas, a fried thick tortilla topped with salsa, shredded meat, chopped onion and queso fresco.

La gente espera deleitarse con platos tradicionales mexicanos como mole poblano y chalupas, una tortilla espesa frita cubierta con salsa, carne desmechada, cebolla picada y queso fresco.

Streets are decorated with the colors of the Mexican flag, red, white and green and crowds enjoy parades throughout the cities.

Las calles están decoradas con los colores de la bandera mexicana, rojo, blanco y verde y las multitudes disfrutan de desfiles por todas las ciudades.

Men and boys wear traditional sombreros while women and girls wear colorful dresses and skirts.

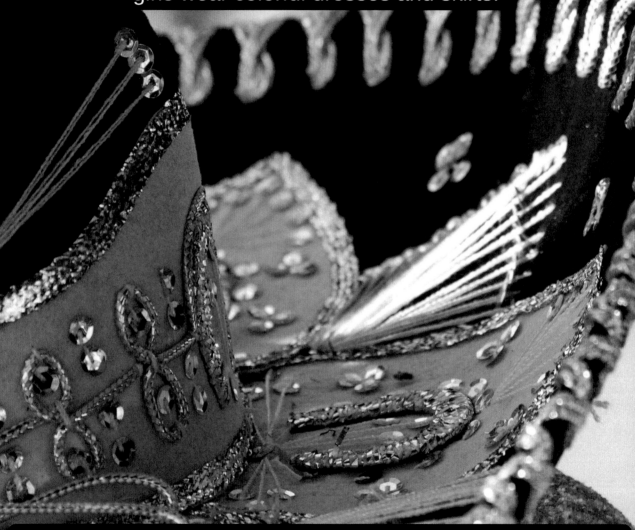

Hombres y niños usan sombreros tradicionales, mientras que las mujeres y las niñas usan vestidos y faldas coloridas.

Children enjoy candy and treats that come from piñatas. Everyone loves taking a swing at the piñata hoping to be the one hit that releases all the sweet treats.

Los niños disfrutan de dulces y golosinas que provienen de las piñatas. A todo el mundo le encanta dar un golpe en la piñata con la esperanza de ser el único golpe que libera todas las golosinas.

It is a very festive time for all who celebrate this holiday! Viva Mexico!

¡Es un momento muy festivo para todos los que celebran esta fiesta! ¡Viva México!

CRAFTS &
COLORING

MAKE YOUR OWN
SARAPE, SOMBRERO, & TACO

Cinco de Mayo
Sarape, Sombrero, and Taco

Supplies:

- Large Paper Bag or Paper Shopping Bag
- Painter's Tape
- Bright Paints
- Paint Brushes
- Pencil
- Glue
- Paper Plate or Palette

Sarape

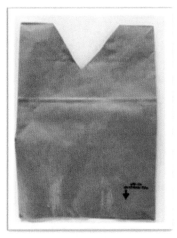

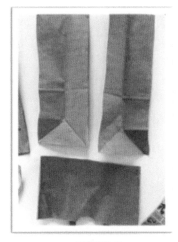

STEP 1
Flatten bag. Cut a triangle out the top to make an opening for the head. Save the triangle to make a TACO

STEP 2
Cut off the two sides of the bag into 2 long pieces. Trim off the extra top of the bag, near the handle. Save these pieces for the hat.

STEP 3
Draw lines across the front of the bag. Paint each section a different color.

STEP 4
When dry, decorate with geometric shapes in contrasting colors.

Sombrero

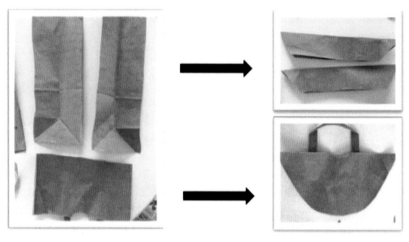

STEP 1
Gather the extra pieces that were left over from the paper bag.

STEP 2
Fold the 2 long pieces in half. Cut the corners off diagonally.
Cut the end piece of the bag into a semicircle. Shape as needed.

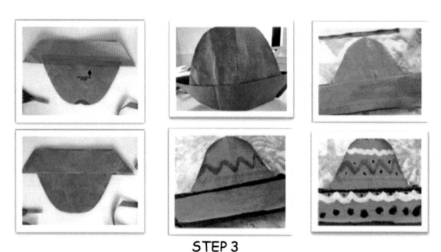

STEP 3
Tape a long strip to each side of the semicircle. Secure ends with tape to form a hat. Paint a solid color and decorate with lines and shapes.

Taco

Taco Shape

STEP 1
Find the triangle that was cut from the top of the bag at the beginning of the project.

STEP 2
Paint the outside yellow. Add brown dots.

STEP 3
Stuff the TACO with scraps of construction paper and shredded paper cheese and lettuce. Glue inside to secure. Looks great!

SENORITA

CHIPS & SALSA

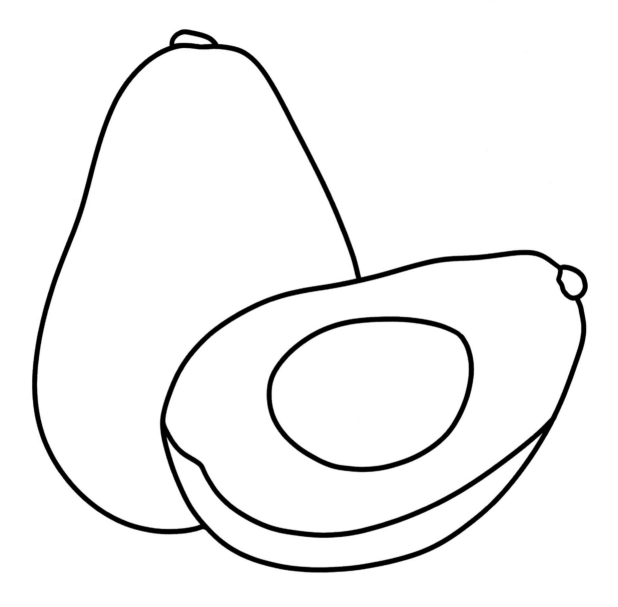

AVOCADO

SARAPE

PIÑATA

MARACAS

GUITAR

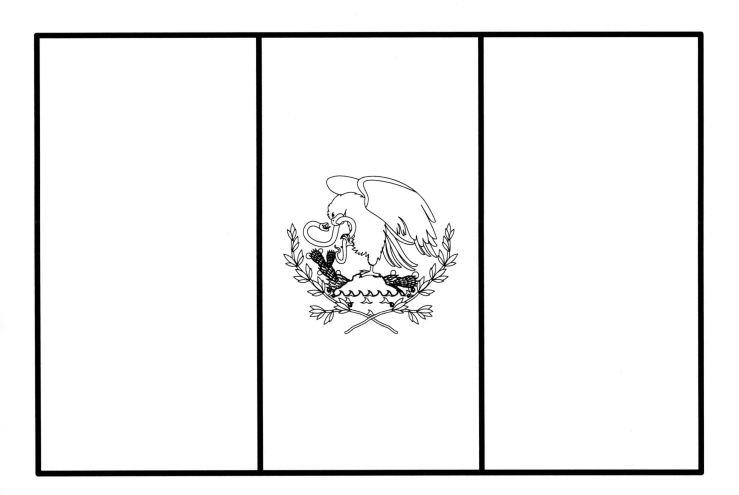

FLAG

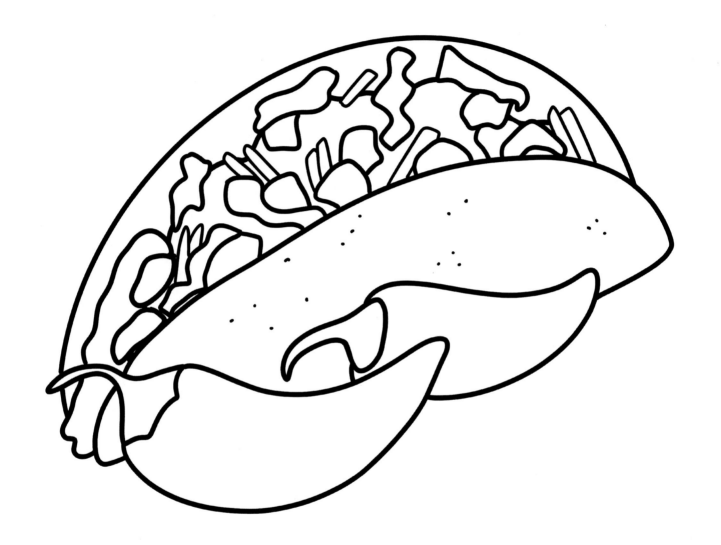

TACO

CACTUS